The Magical Battery Park

Linda Anderson Lieberman

ISBN: 1482391104
ISBN 13: 9781482391107
Library of Congress Control Number: 2013903408
CreateSpace Independent Publishing Platform,
North Charleston, South Carolina

Illustrations by Lorena Soriano

For Jessica, Meghan, Zach, and Peyton,
whose sense of adventure and imagination,
inspired the Magical Battery Park.
And to my husband, a special thank you,
for all your thoughts and funny ideas.

CONTENTS

CHAPTER 1

Kids, Castles, and New York City

"What are we doing today?" Jessica and Meghan asked anxiously as they raced into the living room and grabbed two juice boxes and some fruit off the kitchen counter. The twins were already smartly dressed in their cute play clothes—ready for action.

"It's a great morning to get outside," said Meghan with a sparkling smile as she looked out the windows.

"Good morning to you too," I said, smiling at them as I sipped my tea. "You girls look really adorable in those clothes. Are you thinking of going someplace fancy today?"

"No, I just wanted to wear this outfit on my first day here in New York City, in case I see a cute boy." said Jessica.

"Really, Jessica, get real; there are probably no cute boys here in this city," laughed Meghan. Then she turned to me and pleaded, "Please, Grammy, can we do something fun like go to the Aquarium?" She slid up beside me and gave me a big hug, hoping to persuade me. "You know, the famous Aquarium at Coney Island?"

"Yeah, Grammy!" said Zach as he bolted into the room. He wore his new tie-dyed T-shirt with a spiral design. "That would be awesome. I love aquariums. So many amazing creatures to see, especially the sharks and snakes!"

Jessica, Meghan, and Zach live in Gunnison, a small town high up in the Colorado Rockies. They were visiting their Grampy and me at our home near Battery Park in New York City.

"An aquarium, well, that does sound like fun. But did you know that once upon a time there was a beautiful aquarium right here in Battery Park with hundreds of exotic fish?" I asked, not sure how they would react.

"Grammy, we're not babies anymore; we're twelve years old. We don't do little kids' 'once upon a time' stories anymore," said Meghan, putting her hands on her hips in make-believe frustration.

"Maybe the pipsqueak would like to hear a fairy tale, he's eight," laughed Jessica affectionately, as Zach made a face at her. "Anyway, Grammy, there isn't an aquarium in Battery Park."

"Hmm, it's really not a fairy tale," I said. "It's a real place that's just down the street from us called Castle Clinton. Originally it was a fort. Then it became Castle Garden and later an aquarium. Lots of tourists go there now to get tickets to see the Statue of Liberty. Your great-grandma Judy visited the castle when it was an aquarium. She was about your age girls, maybe a little older."

"Grandma Judy went there?" asked Zach in awe. "Wow, it must be really old!"

"Yes, the castle is old, and Grandma Judy did visit there," I laughed. "Maybe tonight we'll call her and you can ask her what she remembers about the aquarium. How about if we take advantage of the beautiful weather, walk down to Castle Clinton, and find out what happened to this aquarium? Then tomorrow we can go to Coney Island."

"History classes! Yuck, Grammy," the twins sighed in unison, with gloomy looks on their faces.

"We're on vacation," said Jessica.

"Yeah," said Meghan, "we want to have fun, not listen to lectures."

"Well," I said trying not to laugh, "there's a new aquatic carousel in Battery Park called *SeaGlass* with beautiful glass fish. They say it makes you feel like you're in a real aquarium. If you're interested we could go there after we check out Castle Clinton."

Meghan perked up and said, "That might work, if we don't stay too long at a creepy old castle."

"Come on, let's go," said Jessica, pretending to swim like a fish. "I want to get to the carousel to see if I'm in an aquarium, and have an aquatic adventure," she giggled as she swam around the room."

"Me too," yelled Zach, mocking his sister's movements.

Sounding mature, Meghan said, "Really, guys, you've got to be joking, the *SeaGlass* is not an aquarium."

"Okay, you swishy fish," I chuckled as I put down my cup of tea. "Let's finish breakfast. Then we can go explore the 'creepy old castle' before it gets too crowded. Zach, remember what your mom said—stay with your sisters."

"Yeah, unless you want to get lost," scolded Meghan.

"Maybe I'd like getting lost to get away from the two of you," Zach snapped back.

CHAPTER 2

The Creepy Old Castle

It was a sunny morning, and a breeze was blowing gently in Battery Park. A dog was chasing a ball and kids were laughing and playing, while their parents waited in line for the ferryboat to the Statue of Liberty and Ellis Island. A few people were enjoying the warm summer weather, sitting on the benches under the trees. The park looked so inviting with all the beautiful flowers and plants.

Jessica looked around and said, "What a nice day to play in the park. Let's go to the carousel now Grammy, not visit a creepy old castle."

"We'll have time to enjoy the park later, but for now the creepy old castle is waiting for you to explore," I said, steering them toward the building.

"What's there to explore anyway?" Jessica asked, as she and Meghan did cartwheels across the green grass.

"Well for a start, do you see the space over the entrance of the castle doors?" I asked. "If you look closely, you can see where once there were two spectacular golden seahorses welcoming people to the aquarium. Maybe, if you squint your eyes and use your imagination, you'll see them."

"Grammy's gone wacky—there aren't any seahorses on that wall," Meghan whispered to Jessica.

As we entered the castle through the grand wooden doors, Zach glanced over to the thick sandstone walls and whined, "What kind of a castle is this? Where's the dungeon?"

Looking around the circular castle, Jessica piped in, "Doesn't look like an aquarium, either. Where did they keep the fish?"

"Why did they call this place Castle Garden?" Meghan huffed, throwing her hands out in frustration. "It sure doesn't look like the castle we saw in Orlando, and there's no garden in here either."

"Well, there's a park ranger over there who will be leading a guided tour of the castle. Maybe he can answer some of your questions about when it was a fort, castle garden, and the aquarium," I said as I pointed him out. "Wait right here while I go inside the bookstore to sign you up. I'll be right back."

"Hey, at least he's a cute ranger," Jessica whispered to Meghan.

Shaking her head in mock disbelief, Meghan strolled over to the information booth. She picked up a copy of the National Park Service brochure on Castle Clinton.

"Jessica, this will be good to have. I know Grammy will ask lots of questions, and this brochure has all the answers we'll need. Let's look it over before she gets back."

I signed them up for the thirty-minute ranger tour. When I came back to where they were standing, I told them, "When the tour is over, I'll be waiting right here on this circular cistern, where they used to store water. Go, enjoy the tour, but remember, there will be a little test to see what you learned before we head off to the carousel."

Meghan and Jessica looked at each other and laughed.

"Zach," I said, "please stay with your sisters—don't go running off by yourself."

Off they ran to get their questions answered. I knew they were hoping this wouldn't take long so they could get out of the castle and into the park to play. So while they were learning about the castle, I wandered outside for a moment to take a look at the Statue of Liberty and all the boats in the harbor before returning to the cistern to wait for the kids. After what seemed like just a few short minutes, I was brought back to reality by a tug on my arm from Zach.

I glanced up and saw Meghan fluttering around like a butterfly. I laughed and said, "Okay Meghan, you look like you're bursting at the seams to tell me what you learned. So let's hear it—what did the ranger say?"

Looking confident Meghan replied. "The castle has been here for over two hundred years. That's even before Grandma Judy was born. It was built as a fort on a rocky island to keep out the British during the War of 1812."

"They had big cannons too," interrupted Zach. "We got to see one!"

"Zach! I'm talking, let me finish," said Meghan. "Then it became an entertainment center and you had to cross a neat bridge to get there." Then she added excitedly, "Do you know what's amazing, Grammy? The water under the bridge got filled up with dirt and stuff—that's how this area became a park." Looking a little embarrassed she said, "I guess this isn't just a creepy old castle after all."

"Wow, I'm impressed," teased Jessica. "You remembered all that. I was just looking at the cute boy over there who was in our tour."

Meghan just laughed, and said, "That figures. You are always looking at boys."

"Grammy," said Zach impatiently, "do you know Jenny Lynn? The ranger guy said she was a famous singer who came here to make lots of money entertaining people in the castle. He also said you could see lots of new inventions here like the telegraph—even the steam-powered fire engine came here. That's so cool, I wish I could've seen that!"

"Yes, it would've been fun to see all that cool stuff," I replied. "Way to go Zach! I'm so proud of you for remembering so much about this castle."

"Oh yeah, I remember something too," said Jessica, feeling a little left out. "The cute ranger said they needed a place to let lots of new immigrants into our county, so they used this castle for this before Ellis Island was opened. Maybe some of our relatives came through here." Looking at Meghan, she laughed. "See, I can multi-task—looking at boys and listening at the same time, so there!"

"Grammy, I remember something important," boasted Zach. "They closed the em—ma—immigration place, and made the castle into a cool aquarium. So, this wasn't a fairy tale. Lots and lots of people came to see the big fish and animals that lived in pools and tanks here."

"Wow," I said, "so much information. I can tell that all of you were paying attention to the ranger. I'm so glad you learned something about this castle. Not many people even stop to notice the castle, much less find out about its history. You all passed the test," I laughed. "Great job!"

Zach, turned to me and whined, "Enough of this history stuff Grammy. It's so hot, I wish I had a fish pool right now to cool off in, but I'd settle for an ice cream."

"Me too," said Jessica.

"I guess this place really does have a lot of interesting history, but I'm glad that tour is over," said Meghan.

"I'm ready to go see the carousel, and see if I'm in an aquarium," said Jessica. "I'll race you—bet I can get there before you."

As quick as a wink, Jessica and Meghan ran out the front doors of the castle and into the park, leaving Zach behind.

"See Grammy, it's not me who runs away—they ran off without me," sighed Zach.

"Okay, Zach, I'll let them know they shouldn't run off and leave you either. Let's go catch up with the girls; no use in letting them have all the fun." We left the castle and walked into the park.

"Grammy," whispered Zach, "is that a turkey walking through the park? Look over there! What's she doing roaming around here? Turkeys don't live in big cities."

I laughed. "That's Zelda. She's a turkey who has lived here in Battery Park for a few years. She's famous for living in the wild in a big city. Also, there is a turkey-shaped, little urban farm here in the park that was designed in her honor."

With a concerned look on his face, Zach asked, "Where does she go at night, Grammy? Won't she get hit by a car if she goes into the street?"

"Don't worry," I said. "She sleeps in a nest in a tree near the playground, high above the park. She usually comes down early in the morning, and I don't think she wanders too far away from her home. She has lots of human friends who feed her and watch out for her."

"That's so neat, seeing a wild turkey here in this big city," said Zach. "Wait till I get back to Colorado and tell my friends about this!"

Up ahead we could hear Jessica shouting that she could see the carousel. "It's beautiful, and it looks like fish floating in an ocean on land—how enchanting! Hurry up, Zach," she yelled.

Zach took off running, not wanting to be left behind.

CHAPTER 3

The Enchanting Carousel

"Look, Zach," whispered Meghan in a playful spooky voice. "The sign says that all who enter this extraordinary aquatic carousel will ride to the depths of the sea and embark on a magical voyage of excitement." She laughed. "Yeah right, magical, who are they kidding?"

"I wish that I could live in an aquarium with sea creatures for friends. That would be so incredible!" Zach said excitedly.

Somewhere off in the distance, an eel heard Zach's wish.

As Jessica approached the carousel, she stopped. She was in awe and was speechless—a rare event for Jessica. She could hardly take her eyes off the large overhead screens showing the beautiful sea creatures swimming by. The carousel's lights and sounds fascinated her with the bright colors of the fish and moon jellies that moved around the room to the alluring sound of the music.

"Oh my," I said as I caught up with them. "There's no one here. I guess everyone is still at the castle getting tickets for the Statue of Liberty and waiting in those long lines to board the ferryboats. Wow, would you look at those glass fish! They really are beautiful and so colorful. You have the whole carousel to yourselves and all the animals to chose from.

Which fish do you want to ride on Zach? How about you two, which magical animal will you choose?"

"Grammy, they aren't magical. It's just a carousel of fish!" said Meghan. "They're beautiful, but they aren't going to do any magic tricks." Waving her arm and pointing to her brother, she mocked, "Abracadabra, Zach disappear!"

Zach just ignored her. He was so excited about choosing which animal he wanted to ride. He kept looking them over closely, examining each and every one of them, and finally he yelled, "I want the electric eel! He looks like a sea serpent, and I know a lot about electricity. I'm going to name him Sparky."

"I'm getting on the beluga whale," cried Meghan. "She's like me—one of the most intelligent animals on the planet, and she's so beautiful. Hi, Bella. We're going to have a fun ride together."

Jessica, finally coming back to her senses after being mesmerized by the carousel, looked about and said calmly, "I'm riding on the penguin. He looks very handsome in his tux. Maybe we'll go to a royal penguin ball, and he can be my date," she laughed. "I'll call him Peyton, emperor of the penguins."

"You're so silly," said Zach, "naming the penguin after our little brother."

Zach took off to climb up onto the eel's back. Meghan made her way to the beluga whale while Jessica climbed into the tummy of the penguin. They all started laughing with excitement while sitting on their carousel animals.

"Grammy, this is going to be so much fun," said Zach.

"It sure sounds that way," I said. "Hold on, I want to take a picture of all of you to email to your mom. Say cheese."

I took a picture of each of them on their enchanting sea creatures and told them to meet me by the exit door when the ride was over. "And girls, please don't run off and leave your brother like you did a little while ago," I said, as I paid for their tickets. Then I walked outside to watch them ride on their carousel animals, and to look around for Zelda.

Inside, the *SeaGlass* carousel was starting its magical voyage, spinning around the room. Zach, Meghan, and Jessica were thrilled with the sounds of the fish singing:

Swim away, swim away,
Swim away with me,
And you shall see
Creatures of the sea.

The fish started spinning faster and faster. "Hold on tight," cried Zach, "Sparky's trying to swim off this carousal and into the sea."
"Mine too!" yelled Jessica.
"Bella, slow down, we're going too fast!" screamed Meghan.
The sounds of the fish singing grew louder.

Swim away, swim away,
Swim away with me.

They were spinning faster and faster. It felt like they were being sucked into a mysterious whirlpool. Suddenly there was a brilliant flash of light, and Zach, Meghan, and Jessica were off on a magical journey into the deep blue ocean where the creatures of the sea live and play.

CHAPTER 4

The Magical Aquarium

All of a sudden the spinning stopped. The twins found themselves in the middle of a large room. They looked around, not sure what had just happened. One minute they were on the carousel, and the next they were in a large, circular room. Some of the walls were decorated with beautiful murals of fish. Hanging from the ceiling was a stuffed flying fish and a shark. In the center of the room were ten decorated columns that supported arches, which surrounded a large, beautiful pool. Around this pool were six smaller pools filled with wild exotic fish and animals that beckoned them to come closer.

"Where are we?" asked Jessica with a confused look on her face.

"I think we're in an aquarium," said Meghan, bewildered as she looked around, still not believing what she was seeing.

"This place looks familiar," Jessica added nervously. "Seems like we've been here before. It's round like the carousel, with fish too, but this place is so much larger." Glancing around the room, she asked, "How did we get here, and where's Zach?"

"I'm over here," yelled Zach, who was already investigating how he could get over the side of a pool, thinking how good it would feel to be swimming like a fish in one of them.

"Don't run off and get lost," Jessica shouted back at him. "And you better not get into any mischief either." *Zach likes to get up close and personal with all kinds of creatures,* she thought fondly.

Zach just laughed. "This is going to be so much fun," he said to himself as he looked around to see what else was here. He walked over to the tanks that were along the walls and out of sight of his sisters.

Jessica and Meghan moved closer to the center of the large room to take a look at what was inside the grand pool. Along the side of the pool, a chubby black and white penguin waddled toward the girls.

"Can I help you?" asked the penguin. "Are you lost? I can help you find your way around this aquarium."

Jessica and Meghan just stared at each other.

"Am I hearing things Jessica, or did this penguin just talk? No—no way, there must be something wrong with my ears," said Meghan not waiting for an answer from Jessica.

"I think we must be seeing things or dreaming," said Jessica blinking her eyes. "These animals can't be real, can they?"

"What kind of a place is this?" asked Meghan. "Are we in Grammy's fairy tale? This can't be happening."

Realizing that the penguin was waiting for an answer, Jessica replied timidly. "We're not lost. We just got here. I'm not sure where we are, except in a beautiful aquarium."

"I've never seen an aquarium like this before," said Meghan.

Jessica looked closer at the penguin and realized who he was. "Hey, you're my carousel penguin, Peyton, the one I named after my little brother." Then she whispered to herself, "I sure miss him—too bad he couldn't fly on the airplane with us to New York City."

Looking around the room with a perplexed look on her face, Meghan asked, "Where are we? What happened to the carousel?"

"You are in the New York Aquarium," said Peyton the penguin. "And what are you talking about? There are no carousels here in Battery Park in the 1930s," he said with a mischievous sparkle in his eye.

"Oh, but there is a carousel," giggled Jessica. "We were just on one, and you were part of it," she said to the penguin she called Peyton. "I was riding on you, silly penguin."

Meghan chimed in dramatically. "Yes, and this morning we were at Castle Clinton where it was once an aquarium, but the aquarium closed over seventy years ago. So, how can we be there?"

"I can answer your questions," came a pulsating voice from one of the pools. An electric eel stuck his head out of the water. "Zach made a wish to live in an aquarium with sea creatures for friends when he came to the *SeaGlass* carousel. I made his wish come true," he said with a burst of energy.

"Hey, you're Sparky the electric eel and you talk too! This is getting really weird," said Meghan. "See, Peyton, we told you there was a carousel!"

Peyton just laughed making his black and white feathers look puffy and jolly.

"Good grief!" exclaimed Jessica as she looked at Sparky and Peyton. "Have we gone nuts? We're in an aquarium that's been closed over seventy years with talking carousel animals. That's just great!" she said sarcastically, waving her hands around.

"Grammy is going to be really mad that we ran off and didn't tell her," said Meghan. "How in the world will we get back to the carousel?"

"That is a puzzle to be solved. You'll have to figure it out for yourselves," said Peyton the penguin. "I'm sorry, though, Sparky won't be able to wish you back. He can only grant one magical wish."

Sparky slowly slithered back into his pool.

"However," said Peyton, "there are some really clever animals here besides me who may be able to help you find your way back."

"Thank goodness for that," said Jessica.

Then Peyton said sternly. "Stay away from Bertha the barracuda—she is one wretched, mean fish. She would do anything to keep you from getting back on that carousel."

"Oh my," said Meghan, "Bertha the barracuda sounds really scary."

Peyton thought to himself, *I better not tell these girls about Ally the atrocious and dreadful gator; that would really upset them.*

"Meghan," said Jessica softly, "there's a whale right behind you in the pool, and…" Jessica didn't get to finish her sentence, for at that moment, the whale lifted up her head and said, "Please don't be scared, girls. I'm your carousel friend Bella."

"I thought so!" said Meghan, still not believing all of this. "And you talk too, that's brilliant."

"Yes, I do, and I'd like to tell you a little bit about myself," said Bella, hoping to take their minds off Bertha the barracuda. "When I first arrived at the aquarium I was scared. I lived in Canada in the St. Lawrence River. I came by boat just like the immigrants who came here from far away. I was the first beluga whale to be put in an aquarium anywhere. I was terrified too, because I was away from my family and friends."

"I didn't know that," said Meghan with a sad look in her eyes. "I'm really sorry you were taken from your family."

"Don't worry," said Bella, splashing her tail behind her. "It worked out for the best in the end. Just think of this as an adventure for all of us. If we put our heads together, we can figure out a way for you to get back to the carousel. "Besides," she added, "we've never had special visitors like you coming from a different era in time or from a foreign place before, so this will be fun for us too."

"Foreign? Colorado is not a foreign place!" said Jessica as she made a funny face at Bella.

Peyton, who had been thinking about the kids' dilemma, looked at them and said with excitement. "If you explore the aquarium with me, maybe we'll find clues along the way that will help you solve your puzzle."

"That sounds like a great idea. So, where shall we go first?" asked Meghan, thinking that she might as well enjoy this adventure. "I'm ready to explore this old aquarium."

Jessica, realizing that she had not heard a peep from Zach in quite a while, turned to Meghan and asked, "Where's Zach? He needs to come with us too."

"Zach!" shouted Jessica. "Where are you? Stop playing games and get over here."

The girls looked over to the large pool where Zach had been. He was nowhere in sight.

CHAPTER 5

Zach to the Rescue

The adventurous Zach wandered alone down a long, dark corridor that led past the feeding tanks. A fish was in trouble. He was sure he could hear it crying out for help.

"I have to find this fish quickly," he whispered to himself. "Her cries are getting weaker and weaker." Then, Zach thought to himself, *I rescued my cat from a fox back in Colorado, so I know I can rescue a fish. How difficult can it be?*

In the distance, Sparky watched and listened.

Zach continued walking through the mysterious passageway. Along the way, he came upon a pipe that had a sign above it that read, 'Salt water from underground reservoir next to the building.' Zach realized that this pipe must pump water to the tanks, and said bravely to himself, "Maybe I'll follow the pipe and see where it takes me."

Jessica looked about the room, turned to Meghan, and said, "Zach's very inquisitive and likes to discover things on his own. He might get himself into trouble, especially with a miserable fish like Bertha lurking around the aquarium. We need to find him before he has a run-in with that barracuda!"

"Peyton," said Meghan anxiously, "Jessica is right, I'm worried about him. Can you please find him?"

"Don't worry," Peyton said as he turned around toward the large beluga whale's pool. "Bella, we need to find Zach. Can you help?"

"Of course I can," said Bella, moving her head up and down as if she were receiving a signal from someone. "I was just told that he is down by the pumps. Girls, follow Peyton, he knows all the ins and outs of this aquarium."

"You bet I do," said Peyton with a big grin. "This aquarium is filled with the latest 1930s technology and equipment. It has more exquisite fish than any other aquarium in the world. It also has a very complex system of water circulation, aeration, and temperature maintenance necessary for the well-being of the aquarium's ten thousand specimens."

"You sound more like a park ranger tour guide than a penguin," said Meghan. "Please don't tell me you're going to give us history lessons."

"Excellent idea Meghan," said Peyton. "Did you know that this aquarium was once compared to the great temple of Karnack in Egypt, with its huge pillars and great vaulted roof? Cool, huh?" Not waiting for an answer, he continued. "This aquarium has seven large floor pools and ninety-four large wall tanks. Bella the beluga whale's pool is the largest. It is thirty-seven feet in diameter and seven feet deep."

"Wow, you sure do know a lot about this aquarium," Jessica said, looking at Peyton. "I don't know what all that means, but you sure sound amazing."

"Well, I've been here for a few years," said Peyton. "I'm a Galapagos penguin. Did you know that I'm a bird? But, I can't fly like one. I have explored this whole aquarium and I know where things are and how they work. For instance, behind these tanks is a system of catwalks. We can be undercover detectives looking for Zach. I know every nook and cranny here. So, don't you worry, girls, I'll find your brother. Come on, let's go look for him."

Jessica looked from Peyton to Meghan, smiled, and rolled her eyes. "Wow he's cute and a brainiac too!"

"Yeah, I noticed," said Meghan.

"I'm sure you'll find Zach," Bella the beluga whale called out from her pool. "Don't worry, girls, you're in good hands—or flippers—with Peyton," she chuckled as she watch them walk toward the catwalk.

Meanwhile, Zach started to walk faster along the dim passageway as he followed the water pipe. The cries for help were growing weaker and Zach was getting very concerned that the fish was dying—he must get there soon. He turned the corner, and Sparky appeared out of nowhere, scaring Zach so badly that he turned and started to run down the dark corridor.

"Wait!" yelled Sparky. "I'll help you find the fish—I hear her cries too. You must have extraordinary hearing, or did you go into one of the pools and get water in your ears?" he laughed. "Because, the girls can't hear her cries. I didn't mean to frighten you. I'm your friend Sparky from the carousel," he said reassuringly. "Something has cut off the air to a tank, and fish need fresh air in their water or they'll die. Hurry back this way, Zach. We need to get there soon."

Zach stopped and turned around as Sparky flicked his tail. A light in the dark corridor flashed on. "That's so cool," Zach said, as he stared at the eel sliding along the floor. Zach could not believe what he was seeing or hearing—a talking electric eel. He wasn't frightened anymore. He was having fun watching Sparky light up the hallway. "How do you do that?" Zach asked curiously.

"Well," said Sparky, "I'm the electric eel who lives here in the aquarium. I generate enough current to light a bulb over a tank. I have about six thousand specialized cells, called electrocytes. They store power like little batteries. My cells can create a charge of about six hundred volts."

"Wow," said Zach. "Really? Six hundred volts, that's a lot of electricity."

"And, Zach, I know you won't believe this," said Sparky, "but I am an air breathing fish too. That's why I am able to be out of water for a while. I come to the surface regularly to breathe, like a dolphin, but they live mostly in salt water. I live in fresh water rivers. Did you know that I'm one of the most popular fish among the schoolchildren that come to visit this aquarium?" he boasted. "Some think I'm a snake, but I'm not. I'm just a long, skinny, high-voltage fish!"

"Wow, you sure are bright Sparky," said Zach, laughing at his own joke. "I've just got to take you home with me. I have an aquarium at my house that you can live in, and we have lots of fresh water rivers too."

Sparky just laughed.

Meanwhile, Jessica and Meghan followed Peyton along the catwalk, trying not to look worried.

Meghan turned to Jessica and said, "I wonder if Zach's okay? Do you think we'll find him? This aquarium has so many interesting hiding spots, and you know how much Zach loves to play hide and seek."

"Yes, he does," said Jessica. "Let's hope we find him before he finds Bertha the barracuda. But, when I find him, he's in big trouble—making us worry about him. I'm so angry with that little pipsqueak for running off and not telling us. He's got a lot of nerve doing that!"

Meghan laughed, "He might be better off with Bertha the barracuda than with you right now. But, I still hope he's okay."

"Yeah, I'm still worried about him too," said Jessica. "I was just venting off a little steam about him disappearing and not telling us."

CHAPTER 6

Extraordinary Discoveries

Peyton, trying to distract them from thinking about Zach, said, "Look down there girls, and you'll see the small sand shark that lives in one of the pools. Alongside him is a hammerhead shark. His bizarre snout is like a metal detector that sweeps over the bottom of the ocean. His snout can sense the fish buried in sand. But, we'll stay away from him, 'cause he would like to eat me—penguin pizza—now that's scary."

The girls started laughing, thinking about a fish that had a hammer for a head, breaking the tension that they were feeling.

He continued talking. "This aquarium opened in 1896, and was the biggest aquarium in the world with all kinds of exotic sea creatures. Since then, hundreds of thousands of people have come to Battery Park every year to visit this aquarium. It is one of New York City's most popular attractions. Pointing his flipper at the large pool below, Peyton asked, "Girls, what do you see?"

"It's a manatee!" cried Meghan. "Just like the ones we saw in Florida!"

"That's right," said Peyton. "We call her Missy the manatee. Lots of people think she is a mythical mermaid, with a female human head, arms, and body and the tail of a fish. But, she can't turn her head like you and me. When she wants to look around, she has to turn her whole body. Also, she is the only aquatic mammal that is an herbivore; she eats only vegetables—that makes me happy. And when she is underwater she can hear ten times better than you. Now that's what I call 'cool,' cause I like to be 'cool.'" He laughed at his little penguin joke.

The girls thought that Missy didn't look much like Ariel or any other mermaid they'd ever seen. They were really enjoying exploring the sights of the aquarium with their funny tour guide Peyton, but they had not found Zach, and Jessica was still worried.

"Maybe Missy the manatee can help us find Zach," said Jessica, with a hopeful smile. But Missy, who had come up to the surface to breath, didn't say anything. She rolled over lazily and disappeared into her pool.

Peyton continued talking, hoping to get their thoughts on something else. "Look along the walls at the tanks with the wrought iron stands. Do you see all the different smaller fish we have here in the aquarium? One of our most popular fish is the seahorse. Everybody who comes to the aquarium wants to see them. Let's keep moving along so you can see more of our popular fish while we look for Zach."

"Wait," said Jessica. "What can you tell us about those adorable little seahorses?"

"Oh my," said Peyton. "There's a lot to tell about the seahorses. They can majestically glide through the water without any visible effort. They have a transparent fin on their backs that beats twenty to thirty times per second that we can't see."

"A hummingbird flaps its wings like that too," said Meghan with pride that she actually remembered this from science class.

"You're right," said Peyton. "Did you also know that seahorses are able to camouflage themselves in a blink of an eye and rapidly blend in with their surroundings? The seahorses you're looking at are only about six inches tall."

"Wow, and they look like real horses too," said Jessica.

"Oh yeah, girls," said Peyton. "You won't believe this—the male seahorses give birth to the babies.

"That's so neat," said Jessica. "Men having babies," she laughed.

"And girls, another thing you won't believe," said Peyton. "Seahorses used to lived here in the Hudson River, but the river became too polluted for them and they left."

"Maybe one day they'll come back to the river," said Meghan.

"Lets hope so, keep your flippers crossed," laughed Peyton. "Now, look at the tank by the seahorses. Can you see the mud puppies? These are strange sea dogs with external lungs."

The girls looked down and saw the mud puppies. Trying not to laugh, Meghan said. "A dog? Why he's nothing like any dog I've petted or played with, but more like a smooth-skinned lizard. Yuck! Who'd want to pet him?"

Jessica turned to Peyton and teasingly said, "Who gives these creatures such weird names?"

"Uh, well, mud puppies are actually salamanders, and they get their name from the noise they make that sounds like a dog's bark," Peyton stammered as he tried to imitate a dog barking.

"You're very funny, Peyton," said Jessica laughing. "That sounds more like a goose honking, than a dog barking."

"Well, we have another friend who can bark like a dog, and he is very loud when he barks. He came to the aquarium when he was only two," said Peyton timidly, afraid they would laugh at him again.

"Only two, wow, that's young!" said Meghan. "Who is this barking friend, another strange sea dog?"

"No," laughed Peyton, "he's our sea lion named Buster. Look down over there by the side of the pool below us. Can you see him? He is always looking for a handout, and boy does he love fish."

"Well, Buster, should be very happy in this aquarium; there are lots of fish here!" said Meghan.

"Yes, listen to him bark. He is especially loud when he wants more fish! Oh no, he sees you, and thinks you'll throw him one," said Peyton.

"Yeah right," said Jessica. "Like I carry fish in my pocket, silly Buster."

"Well, keep moving along, girls. We must find Zach," Peyton reminded them.

"He's such a drill sergeant," Jessica said to Meghan.

"I heard that. Hup, two, three, four," said Peyton laughing.

They continued along on the catwalk, hoping to find something that would lead them to Zach.

Soon, they were passing by the octopus tank. Meghan made a funny face and pointed to it. "That looks like a large domed head sitting on top of swirling legs, like a giant spider," she teased, "but with fatter legs."

"Actually, that's an octopus," laughed Peyton. "Her head is called the mantle or body and contains all of the octopus's vital organs—including three hearts. She also has a well-developed brain and can negotiate mazes, solve puzzles, and distinguish between shapes and patterns. Girls, I'd like you to meet Venus, our resident scholar."

"Three hearts," sighed Jessica. "I could use three hearts to fall in love with three different boys at once," she laughed.

Venus was delighted to see Jessica laugh; she knew Jessica was anxious about Zach.

"Really, Jessica! Get over it," said Meghan. "We need her help to find Zach, and maybe, she'll solve our puzzle too. It's nice to meet you, Venus. Sorry, my sister is boy crazy."

Jessica, realizing that Meghan was right, looked around to see if there was something that could help them find Zach. "Look! Over there, I see something," Jessica said to Meghan, as she walked over to see what it was; hoping it was something Zach had dropped. It was a small booklet. She picked it up and stared at it, not believing what she was holding.

"Oh my goodness," said Jessica. "It's *A Guide to the New York Aquarium*, and it's really old. I don't think Zach dropped this. Meghan, it has seahorses on the cover. Maybe there is something in this book that can help us get home." She noticed the name Judith written on the cover as she handed it to Meghan to look at.

Meghan took the book and said excitedly, "Maybe there's a clue in it. Look, there's a loose page with notes written on it. Let me see what it says." Then she read the note to Jessica.

Life is an adventure, go and explore the aquarium, for when you reach the end, you will arrive from where you started. But remember the most wonderful places lie within your imagination; follow your heart's desires.

"Is this some kind of clue for us to keep on exploring to the end so that we can arrive where we started? What does that mean?" asked Jessica with a confused look upon her face.

"Venus, can this book help us get home?" asked Meghan.

"Oh yes," said Venus. "The way home is looking right at you. Look closely at what you see and read. This will show you the way."

"That's wonderful," said Peyton to everyone anxiously. "Let's keep that in mind, but for now we need to find Zach. Hopefully he hasn't met up with Bertha the barracuda."

Meanwhile, Zach and Sparky moved quickly along the corridor. They were still hearing the cries of a terrified fish. "Let's go this way, Zach," said Sparky. "We're nearly there." He looked straight ahead into the large fish tank and groaned, "Oh No! It's Bertha who's crying."

CHAPTER 7

The Wretched and Wonderful Barracuda

"Peyton, why is Bertha the barracuda such a problem?" asked Jessica innocently. "Isn't she a magical fish too?"

"Oh," said Peyton, "Bertha is a despicable fish. She is bold and fearsome. She lies in wait to catch her prey by surprise. Her torpedo shaped body gives her speed to ambush them. Also, Bertha has no eyelids, and hunts by sight. I nicknamed her 'Tiger of the Sea' because she has a big toothy grin."

Jessica laughed, "Another silly name for a fish. Lots of teeth but no eyelids, I guess she doesn't sleep much."

"But she does, don't let her eyes fool you," said Peyton. "And another interesting thing about Bertha is her gas-filled swim bladder. It's like a balloon that she can inflate or deflate to rise up or swim deeper."

"That's amazing, but can't every fish do that?" questioned Meghan.

"No," said Peyton, "only the bony fish. Lots of fish have cartilage, instead of bones, like the shark for example—but let's not talk about him right now."

"Where is Bertha?" Jessica chimed in.

"She lives in one of the big fish tanks along the walls, and we are just about there," said Peyton.

"Oh my," said Jessica faintly. "She sounds awful. Zach won't know she's a mean fish, and might get hurt."

Zach and Sparky were looking into the tank when Meghan, Jessica, and Peyton showed up.

"Zach," yelled Jessica, "where've you been? You are in so much trouble. You should have told us you were wandering off. You little pipsqueak, you know better."

Zach slowly whispered. "Sorry, I wasn't thinking, I kept hearing a fish cry and I needed to find it. But, Meghan, Jessica, you won't believe this—Sparky talks and can make electricity with his body."

The girls burst out laughing!

"It's not funny!" yelled Zach. "He really can!"

"Yes, we know," said Meghan. "He's a magical fish that lives here in the aquarium. He made your wish come true."

"Here, meet Peyton the penguin—he talks too," said Jessica.

"What wish?" said Zach to Meghan while glancing suspiciously at Peyton.

"You know, the one where you said you wished you could live in an aquarium with sea creatures for friends. Sparky granted your wish and here we are," said Meghan as she hugged Zach.

"You talk too? Really?" asked Zach, now staring at the penguin.

"Yep," said Peyton.

"He talks as much as our little brother Peyton, who never shuts up," said Jessica, "But he has a lot more interesting things to say."

Zach laughed as he thought about his brother Peyton. He sure loves to talk, and he certainly never shuts up. Jessica calls him a chatterbox—he even talks in his sleep.

"Okay, so what's wrong with Bertha the barracuda?" asked Peyton, seeing the look of distress on her face.

"She's having trouble breathing," said Sparky. "There isn't enough air in her water. Look at her; she is at the surface with her mouth open trying to get air. Something must be wrong with the aeration system."

"How can we help?" asked Meghan.

"She can't die!" yelled Zach.

"You need to find out what has jammed her airflow," said Sparky. "Open up the lid to her tank. Look inside for anything that is blocking the air coming into the tank."

"I can do that," said Zach. "Help me climb up, Meghan."

But at that moment, Bertha the barracuda started to sink.

"Quick, Zach, she's sinking and will drown if we don't get air into her tank," cried Jessica.

Zach hurried up onto the top of the tank and opened the large lid. He found a starfish caught in the air tube.

"It's a starfish!" Zach yelled out. "It's stuck, but if I move him he'll loose an arm and he might die too."

"Don't worry," said Peyton. "Starfish don't have brains, but they have eyes, one at the end of each leg. If a starfish is torn in two, or looses a leg, he'll regenerate himself and develop into two perfectly formed starfish."

"Zach," shouted Meghan, "he'll grow back a new arm, and he won't die. Just pull him off the opening of the tube so the air can flow again."

Quickly Zach yanked the starfish off the opening of the air tube, losing his balance and falling into the water. Soon the air was reaching Bertha and she started to rise from the bottom of the tank.

Breathing deeply, Bertha whispered in a weak voice, "Who is in my tank?"

Peyton quickly said, "Bertha, this is Zach, he rescued you. You should thank him. You would have drowned if it weren't for Zach."

Bertha the barracuda looked over at Zach and said, "Is this true—did you save me?"

Zach didn't know what to say; he just nodded his head. He was glad the fish hadn't died, and besides, he was enjoying swimming in Bertha's large tank.

"Thank you," said Bertha. "You are my special friend, and I owe you a favor."

Sparky, seeing that Zach had rescued Bertha, slithered away to find his home. He had been out of the water too long, and his batteries were getting very low.

Jessica helped Zach get out of the pool and said, "You're lucky, Zach, that Bertha didn't take a bite out of you. She's not a very nice fish most of the time, but I'm glad you rescued her."

"Me too," said Zach, who was soaking wet.

"But, Zach," continued Jessica, "You had us worried when we couldn't find you. Please don't run off and not tell anyone ever again!"

"I promise I'll try to remember," said Zach. "But, sometimes I forget when there are   so many fun things to see and do." He turned around so no   one could hear him, and whispered softly, "I'm sorry, little starfish, for hurting you." Then he handed the starfish to Peyton, and said, "Please keep him safe so he can grow back his arm."

Peyton took the starfish from Zach and assured him that the he would be as good as new in a few weeks. Then he told Zach that Bertha the barracuda was so grateful that he had rescued her, that she would be his special guardian fish.

Peyton turned around to the others and said, "Come on, let's go find Bella; she'll want to see that Zach's okay."

They all ran along the catwalk and down the stairs into the beautiful large room with the shark hanging from the ceiling.

Bella the beluga whale was anxiously waiting for them in the center of the room in the large pool.

"Hi, Bella," yelled Meghan. "I'm so glad to see you again."

CHAPTER 8

Magical Entertainment

Bella the beluga whale was so excited to see the kids all together again, and wanted to tell them about a funny thing that happened here at the aquarium. She hoped it would help them forget about solving their puzzle for a little while.

"Hey everyone," said Bella. "Did you know that we have a famous entertainer in our midst? Really, we do. A few years ago, they made a movie here at the aquarium over by the penguin pool, and our friend Peyton was a star."

Peyton, not wanting to hear about his movie days, walked over to the tanks along the wall. He was embarrassed by all this fuss about him, and tried to hide.

"I didn't know there were movies that old," said Jessica laughing. "Did he talk as much as he does now?"

"No," said Bella, as she dove into the deep pool. She quickly jumped up, spouting water everywhere and said laughing, "He didn't talk at all."

"No way! Really? That's funny," said Meghan. "Who would have thought?"

"Yea, that's hard to believe," laughed Jessica. "And, Bella, that's a lot of water coming out of your blowhole!"

"Sorry, Jessica, I wasn't trying to get you wet," laughed Bella.

"I know you weren't, but I'm getting away from your splashes," said Jessica. Then she turned to Meghan "I'm going to see what's in those tanks under the big hanging shark. I won't get wet there and ruin my outfit," she laughed.

"Okay miss prissy pants," teased Meghan. "Stay dry!"

"And don't run off," said Zach laughing.

Bella swam over to the side of the pool and said, "Meghan or Zach, would you like to ride on me while I swim backwards? I'm the only whale that can swim backwards and I can move my head from side to side. Look at my dorsal fin—don't see one do you?" she laughed. "That's because I don't have one like most whales."

"Bella," said Meghan, "you're different from other whales I've seen in books, and so cuddly. I would love to wrap my arms around you, just like I did on the carousel."

Realizing that Meghan was starting to think about getting home, Bella swam backwards and said, "I love to sing too—I sing like a canary." Bella laughed and started to sing.

Zach thought that was hilarious, a whale that sings like a bird. Just then a scallop wanted to get Zach's attention; he was a hero for rescuing Bertha the barracuda.

"Look at me, Zach!" clapped the scallop, as he swam by at jet-propelled speed. "I can swim really fast when I clap my shell open and shut."

"Whoa! You sure are fast!" shouted Zach. "Hey Meghan, come see this scallop swimming around this pool. I can hardly keep up with him, can you?"

Meanwhile, Jessica strolled over to one of the tanks along the wall, and admired a beautiful shell, floating silently in the blue water. This shell fascinated her.

"Jessica, meet Shelby the chambered nautilus," said Peyton, coming out of his hiding place. He walked nearer to her and said, "He is a cephalopod, and he's shy. If you look closely, you can see that his shell is made of many individual chambers. Each chamber is sealed and contains a small amount of gas. This helps him stay afloat. His strong shell provides protection for his soft body. He's kind of like the hermit crab, but he doesn't crawl around on stuff."

"I had a hermit crab once," said Jessica sadly. "I called him Sandy because he liked to hide from me in the sand."

Jessica looked away from Shelby the chambered nautilus and turned to face Peyton. "Why didn't you tell us you were famous?"

Peyton blushed. "Oh, I didn't think it was important," he said modestly and changed the subject. "Can you see the swirls that make up Shelby's nautilus shell? Look closely and you can see that it's the same shape as the spiral on Zach's T-shirt. Did you know that you could see this same spiral shape in outer space in some galaxies and in hurricanes? It's called a logarithmic spiral pattern."

"That's amazing! A logarithmic spiral pattern," said Jessica. "I like the sound of these new words." Looking at Peyton, she said, "I think the *SeaGlass* carousel has the same design as Shelby's nautilus shell. Let's find Zach and Meghan and show them Shelby. Maybe it's a clue too."

"Okay," said Peyton deep in thought, not realizing he was walking toward the shark pool. Jessica followed slowly. She was still wondering how they would get back to the carousel and was trying to put some of the clues together, but not having much luck.

Zach and Meghan were still at Bella's large pool. Looking around the room, Meghan saw splashing in one of the small oblong pools that surrounded Bella's large pool.

"Zach, I'm tired of running around this pool chasing the scallop," she said. "I'm going to see what is in that pool over there; want to come with me?"

"Nope," said Zach, "I'm going to watch this funny little scallop a little while longer and then I'm going to find the shark pool. Don't worry, I won't get lost, I'll stay where you can see me."

"Okay," said Meghan, and she walked over to the oblong pool and looked inside.

A playful porpoise was moving about the pool in various directions, racing at a high speed. Just then, he leaped up to the surface and started swimming belly up, smacking the surface of the water with its tail.

"Yikes," Meghan yelled. "You soaked me, it's a good thing Jessica's not with me," she chuckled.

The porpoise laughed with delight.

"Are you a dolphin?" Meghan asked as she tried to rub his tummy.

"No, I'm a porpoise, little boy," he said playfully to Meghan.

"I'm not a boy," Meghan said, realizing that he was teasing her.

The porpoise smiled as he turned over in the water to talk to her. "Lots of people confuse us porpoises with dolphins, but I'm different. I'm shorter and more compact. My fin on my back is more triangular in shape than the dolphin's fin, which is curved like a wave. Look at my face, and you can that see my nose is shorter. Dolphins have noses like Pinocchio!" the porpoise laughed.

"Yes," said Meghan, "I can see that now. I don't know much about porpoises. Most of the aquariums I've seen have dolphins in them. Where do you come from?"

"Well, I was born off the coast of Hatteras, North Carolina. I've been here for a couple of years, and I too was separated from my family," the porpoise said.

"I'm sorry I called you a dolphin," said Meghan. "But you are still fun to watch, and I really enjoyed your show, even though you got me wet," she teased.

"Well, just watch how high I can jump," said the porpoise.

He sped off to the other side of the pool, leaving Meghan in awe as she watched him jump high out of the water. Looking around the room, she walked toward another pool, wondering what she would find when she got there.

After watching the scallop disappear into the deep end of the pool; Zach ran over to the shark pool and yelled, "Oh my gosh! That's the weirdest looking shark I've ever seen—his eyes are on his nose."

"Zach, you're so silly, that's not his nose," said Peyton, as he doubled over laughing at Zach's description of the shark. Then looking around, he realized that he had wandered over to the shark pool—the one pool he wanted to stay away from.

"It's not funny!" yelled Zach. "I've never seen a shark like that before."

"Sorry, I forgot you're from Colorado," said Peyton. "That's his funny looking head and it's flat like a hammer. That's where he gets his name, hammerhead, but don't get any funny ideas about getting in his pool to pet him. Let's get away from here, he's a scary shark."

Just then the shark with the funny head swam up to the side of the pool and said, "Little boy, let me take a closer look at you. Climb into my pool and swim with me. I won't hurt you. I promise. I'd like to invite you for dinner."

"No way," said Zach. "You're the big bad wolf in water with sharp teeth, and you'll eat me. I'm outta here," and he looked around for Meghan.

"Hey, Zach, look over here," yelled Meghan. "There's a giant turtle in this pool, but it doesn't have much water. This pool has steps so the turtle can climb to the top and rest where everybody can see him. I wonder if we can ride on this huge turtle?"

"That sounds like fun; I've never been on a turtle before. How big is he?" asked Zach. "Can we both fit on him?" And he ran quickly over to the turtle's pool.

"No!" yelled Peyton to the kids. "For goodness sake, don't get in that pool! Ally the gator is in there with the turtle. You don't want to be in the pool with him lurking about waiting to eat anything that comes his way. Only his eyes and nostrils can be seen and he'll quickly attack you as soon as you put your foot over the edge of the pool."

"Great! Another animal that wants to eat me," Zach laughed. "Come on Meghan, let's get away from here. That doesn't sound like fun. Although, it would have been awesome to ride on a turtle."

"No way, don't even think about it," said Meghan. "We're not going to be lunch for a wicked animal, just to ride the turtle. I'll wait till it's safe. Let's go find Jessica."

Peyton was troubled; he did not want to scare the kids. Ally the gator was more dangerous than Bertha the barracuda. Ally was a large creature with amazing strength and a powerful tail. His bite could crush a child, and he was a fast swimmer. *Hmm,* Peyton thought to himself, *as long as I can keep them away from Ally's pool, they should be okay.* But, he was still worried. If Ally got out of his pool, he would be a danger to the kids. Ally was a cruel creature.

As Meghan and Zach left to look for Jessica, a loud growling sound could be heard coming from the pool.

"Hey, Jessica, what are you doing over there?" Meghan called out. "Didn't get wet did you?" she laughed.

Zach, pretending to be mad at her yelled, "And just where have you been?"

Jessica was so fascinated with the aquarium. She looked around the beautiful room, and said to them, "This reminds me of what the ranger said about Castle Garden when it was an entertainment center. Remember he said famous people put on shows; but now, magical animals are entertaining us," she laughed.

Meghan and Zach ran up to her, and Zach said, "Yeah, and I guess you think we are immigrants coming from a foreign place, but I'm getting hungry, and Grammy promised us ice cream. I'm ready to get back on the carousel and see her."

"Me too," said Meghan wearily. "It's time to solve this puzzle and find our way back."

Jessica said sadly, "Okay, I'm ready too. Meghan, do you still have that guidebook to the aquarium?"

"I left it with Bella," said Meghan. "Don't worry, Jessica, our friends will help us get back. I just know they will."

"Why do we need a guidebook to get us back to the carousel?" Zach asked curiously as they walked toward the center of the large room. "Can't Sparky just wish us back?"

"No, he can't," Meghan told Zach. "Sparky can only grant one wish, and Peyton said we have to solve the puzzle by ourselves to get back home. We have to find clues that will show us the way."

"But don't worry, Zach, the magical animals will help us once we find the clues. Come on, let's find Bella," said Meghan.

CHAPTER 9

The Golden Seahorses

Meghan walked over to the beluga whale's grand pool and said, "Bella, we need the guidebook I left with you. Venus said it would show us the way home."

"It's on the other side of my pool out of the way of my splashes," said Bella, as she swam up to Meghan hoping to get a big hug.

Meghan hugged Bella, and then ran over and picked up the guidebook. She turned to Jessica and said anxiously, "I hope the clues in this book will help us solve our puzzle."

"Don't worry, you'll find your way back," said Peyton, grinning as he casually walked over to them, "Or someone will create a way for you to get back. We'll all help you once you find the clues. But, it is wise to ask Venus the octopus what it is you are looking for before you begin to look for it."

Venus, hearing her name, looked down from her tank and said to them, "First, look closely at the guidebook. What do you see? Then close your eyes and imagine where you want to be. Wish with all your heart."

"I see seahorses," yelled Zach as he looked at the booklet. "How will they help us get back?"

"The golden seahorses on the door to the future are waiting for you. You must find them," said Venus. Then she added cautiously, "You must go boldly in the direction of the one who lies in wait for you. If you follow your heart's desires, you will make it safely to where you started."

"I hope she's not talking about Bertha the barracuda," Meghan whispered to Jessica, not wanting Zach to hear. "Peyton did tell us she lies in wait to catch her prey by surprise, and she's wretched. Even if she does owe Zach a favor, she doesn't owe us one."

"That's true," said Jessica. "We'll have to stay away from Bertha the barracuda while we look for the golden seahorses."

"Okay," said Zach, looking at Peyton, not hearing or caring what the girls were whispering. "So where are the seahorses?"

"That is the puzzle you will have to solve by yourself," said Peyton.

"Well," said Jessica, looking upset. "Where shall we begin? We've already explored the aquarium with you, Peyton, and didn't find those seahorses that Venus told us about. And where is the door to the future?"

Meghan then opened the guidebook, found the loose page, and looked again at the note.

Life is an adventure, go out and explore the aquarium, for when you reach the end, you will arrive from where you started. But remember that the most wonderful places lie within your imagination; follow your heart's desires.

"I've got it," said Meghan, as she put the booklet in the pocket of her pants. "Remember Venus told us to close our eyes and imagine where we want to be? Well, lets try it now. As Venus said, "Where do we want to be?"

"Back on the carousel," said Zach.

"Me too," whispered the girls in unison.

They all closed their eyes and imagined where they wanted to be, hoping that when they opened them, they would be back on the carousel. But when they opened their eyes, they were still in the aquarium.

"That was too easy," said Jessica hopelessly. "And it didn't work!"

"No, we're still here and not on the carousel," said Zach looking worried. "What did we do wrong?"

"Well, let's go over our clues," Meghan urged them. "The first clue is the guidebook with the seahorses on the cover. Venus said they are on the door to the future. Then the note inside said when we reach the end, we will arrive from where we started. Then something about imagination and hearts' desires. Let's start with the seahorses."

"Where are these seahorses?" asked Jessica. "We've explored the whole aquarium, and the only ones we saw were the small ones in a tank. So, where is the end and the door to the future?" she said sounding very frustrated. Just as she was thinking about the seahorses, she wondered out loud, "Didn't Grammy say something about seahorses when we were going into the castle this morning?"

"You're right," said Meghan. "Grammy told us that if we looked closely above the entrance to the castle—The door!" she exclaimed. "They're outside, the golden seahorses are outside! That's where we started this morning, so it must be the door to the end of our adventure."

"I bet it's the door to the future!" said Zach.

Meghan was so excited she danced and did cartwheels around the room. Finally they would see the magical seahorses that would get them back to the carousel.

Jessica was so relieved that they soon would be going back to the *SeaGlass* carousel that she walked over and gave Peyton a great big kiss on the cheek. He turned bright red and started walking timidly toward the middle of the room with a wobble in his waddle.

"Poor Peyton," said Zach. "I don't think he likes to be kissed; he seems a bit lost." Then he added, "Me too! I'm a bit turned around in this big circular place. Where is the entrance to the aquarium? We need to hunt down those seahorses."

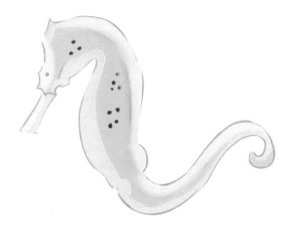

CHAPTER 10

Trouble at the Door

Back in the reptile pool, the gator growled. He was still angry that Peyton had warned the kids to stay away from him. *They will never find those seahorses*, he thought as he lurked beneath the surface with only his eyes out of the water.

"I will find a way to stop them," Ally the gator said wickedly to himself.

He then swam closer to the stairs and started climbing up and out over the edge of the pool. He made his way down to the entrance of the aquarium and found a place to hide.

At that moment, there was a loud buzz of chattering among all the fish and animals throughout the aquarium. They were worried about the kids getting back to the carousel, especially with Ally lurking in the shadows. They knew he was determined to stop them.

Bella the beluga whale stopped swimming. She was receiving signals that Ally was on the prowl. She must let Peyton and the others know the kids were in danger.

Bertha the barracuda hearing the news about the gator, knew the path to the seahorses would be dangerous. Their nemesis, Ally the gator could harm her friend, Zach, and she was determined not to let that happen.

On the other side of the room, Sparky the electric eel was waiting anxiously for Zach to return. His batteries were charged, but he did not like the rumors that were sizzling through his body.

Jessica, Meghan, and Zach left the middle of the room and started walking around the circular walls. They were excited about finding the seahorses and getting back to the carousel. When they reached the doorway to the outside, they saw a large alligator lying between them and the doors.

Meghan suddenly remembered what Venus had told them: *Stay away from trouble that lies in your path, and you will make it safely to where you started.* She whispered to Jessica, "Ally the gator is the trouble that Venus warned us about that would lie in our path, not Bertha the barracuda."

"Looking for something?" asked Ally the gator, as he blocked the exit door.

"Nothing that concerns you," said Zach. "So move out of our way," he said boldly.

"You concern me, and I'm not moving," said the evil Ally. "You will not make it out this door. I will take you back to my lair and have you for lunch and dinner. You look mighty tasty, and no one will miss you. Nobody even knows where you are."

"Meghan, what can we to do about him? He does look like trouble, how will we get through the door?" Jessica asked nervously.

Meghan was deep in thought. She had an idea. "Jessica, we could use our gymnastics to divert him, but we'll have to be quick."

"Do you think we'll be able to outsmart him with gymnastics tricks?" asked Jessica doubtfully.

"I don't think gators are very brainy," said Meghan. "So, maybe we can, and he probably can't move very fast either."

"I guess we have to try something," said Jessica. "He looks frightful and mean, I hope this works."

"Okay, Zach," said Meghan. "Jessica and I are going to distract him, so you can get through the door and out to the seahorses."

But, just as Jessica and Meghan were about to sidetrack the gator, Bertha the barracuda bellowed out from her pool.

"Ally, go back to your lair, and let Zach find the seahorses. You can have me for lunch if you let him pass—besides, he doesn't taste as good as I do," Bertha taunted him.

At that moment, the gator growled. He did not like being taunted. "Well, I have been wanting a large tasty fish for lunch," said Ally, and he moved quickly toward Bertha's pool.

"Whew, we were lucky; he does move pretty fast after all. Thank goodness for Bertha, or we might be down in his lair right now," said Jessica.

"I think Bertha outsmarted him," said Meghan. "How will he get into her pool? There are no steps. Can't you just imagine him trying to climb up the side of her pool?" she joked.

They were all glad that Ally was out of the doorway. They started laughing at the thought of him trying to get into Bertha's pool.

Meghan, Jessica, and Zach then ran quickly through the door where they had started that morning. They looked at the space over the entrance of the castle doors, and lo and behold, there they were, the golden seahorses waiting for them.

"They're just like Grammy described them," said Meghan. "The beautiful golden seahorses."

At that moment Peyton, who was back to his old self, arrived through the door.

"Sugar and Spice, may I present Zach, Meghan, and Jessica? They need to return to the *SeaGlass* carousel. Will you lead the way and become a part of the beautiful carousel?" asked Peyton.

Looking at each other, the seahorses raised their heads and said, "Of course, we'll be delighted to help them reach the carousel. Are you ready to go?"

The seahorses leaped down and told the kids to jump onto their backs. A big sigh of relief came from all of them.

But Peyton interrupted, "We're not quite ready to go, Sugar and Spice. We must all go back inside the aquarium, where Bella and Sparky are waiting. They want to come with us too. And I have a special mission to take care of before we can leave."

CHAPTER 11

The Magical Journey Home

Bella the beluga whale, and Sparky the electric eel, were waiting patiently inside for the kids along with the seahorses Sugar and Spice, who were a little sad to be leaving this magical aquarium. They had enjoyed sitting atop the entrance to the castle door, welcoming those coming to the aquarium. But, they knew it would be more fun to become beautiful fish at the entrance to the *SeaGlass* carousel. They looked anxiously at Bella and Sparky, thinking about the new adventure they were about to begin.

Jessica, Meghan, and Zach were hurrying through the aquarium to say goodbye to all their new friends. Bella had told them that Ally the gator was back in his pool sulking and wouldn't harm them—they would be safe. The girls went to see Venus the octopus to thank her for her help. Zach especially wanted to thank Bertha the barracuda for getting the gator out of his way and to make sure she was okay.

They quickly said their goodbyes and returned to where the magical fish and animals were waiting. They would miss the beautiful aquarium and all the friends they were leaving behind, but they were anxious to leave and be back in Battery Park. Just then, Peyton walked up and reminded Jessica that they must go see Shelby.

"Oh yes, Shelby the chambered nautilus," Jessica said, remembering that Meghan and Zach had not met him yet. "But why do we need to see him now? We are all ready to leave. Can't we just tell Meghan and Zach about him later? Everyone is waiting for us."

"Remember I told you I had a special mission to take care of? Well, I went to see Shelby, and he agreed to create a way for us to get back to the carousel once you found the clues and solved the puzzle," Peyton said cheerfully.

Peyton explained that Shelby with his "amazing spiral" would transport them back to the *SeaGlass* carousel through his magical swirls. "When we arrive back, Shelby will become part of the *SeaGlass* carousel too. Follow me, kids," he said fearlessly, "So we can be on our way."

Following Peyton, they all arrived at the tank that held the cephalopod.

"Meghan, Zach, this is Shelby the chambered nautilus. He lives in a magical nautilus shell and will start a spiral like the one on your T-shirt Zach, and on his shell. Shelby, are you ready?" Peyton asked.

"Yes, Peyton, I'm ready," replied Shelby.

"Bella, are you set to go? Sparky, are your batteries charged? Sugar and Spice, ready to lead the way?" Peyton asked the magical animals.

"Yes!" said the magical animals.

"It's been so much fun and a little scary here at this aquarium," Meghan said to Jessica and Zach.

"Yes it has," said Jessica who turned toward Zach and said, "I can't believe you weren't scared of Ally or Bertha. You're one brave little pipsqueak. But, don't wander off again!"

"No way!" said Zach, "I've had enough excitement for one day."

"Well, Zach, are you up for one more fun ride?" asked Meghan. "Because, I think Shelby's miraculous spiral is about to begin."

"Jessica, Meghan, Zach, climb on your friends and get set for another magical journey back to the aquatic carousel," commanded Peyton.

"There he goes sounding like a drill sergeant again," said Meghan, "but that's okay, I'm ready to go." Then she walked toward Bella's pool, and climbed up on her back. She snuggled closely to Bella and whispered, "It's good to hug you again."

Zach took a running start, slid up onto Sparky, and said, "Hey, buddy, wish I could bring you back to Colorado with me." Sparky started to glow.

Jessica waited for Peyton to take his place. Then she hugged him and held on with all her might. She whispered to him, "thank you Peyton, this was truly an amazing adventure."

"Ready everyone? Hold on tight," said Shelby, squeamishly. "This may be a little shaky, but we'll make it."

"One more thing!" exclaimed Peyton. "The last clue. Close your eyes and use your imagination. Like Venus said, wish with all your hearts' desires to get us safely back to the *SeaGlass* carousel."

"Oops," said Jessica, "we were supposed to wish with all our heart's desire to be back on the carousel."

"Of course!" said Meghan, "I forgot about that part, that's why it didn't work. Venus, thank you again for helping us figure out the clues to our puzzle."

"Oh Venus," sighed Jessica, "you're so lucky to have three hearts."

"Travel safe, my friends," whispered Venus as she watch from above. "I will miss you." Then she laughed, "with all my three hearts."

"Sugar and Spice, lead the way," cried Peyton.

"Goodbye, everyone," they yelled, holding on tight to their magical animals. They all closed their eyes and, using their hearts' desires, wished to be back on the carousel.

Round and round they went in Shelby's spiral. Spinning faster and faster, swirling and twirling while in the distance they could hear singing:

Swim away, swim away
Swim away with me
Swim away into
The deep blue sea.

They were off again on a magical journey, descending deep into the blue sea where the magical creatures lived. In a twinkle of a starfish's eyes, the miraculous spiral swirls returned them back to the *SeaGlass* carousel. Sparky, Bella, and Peyton became beautiful carousel animals again. Two new additions, Sugar and Spice, elegantly adorned the entrance to welcome everyone.

CHAPTER 12

The Spirals in Battery Park

"Grammy, Grammy, you have to come meet our new friends," they all yelled as they ran out the exit door toward me all excited about the carousel ride.

"What new friends are you talking about? Where are they?" I asked curiously, looking about the area. "I thought you were the only ones on the carousel."

"You'll see," they said, as they took my arm and pulled me inside.

"There are no kids here," I said. "Maybe they are with their parents. Let's go back outside and see. Maybe we missed them while we were coming back into the carousel."

"No, Grammy. Remember, there were no kids on the carousel with us. These are our new friends, Sugar and Spice, Bella, Sparky, and Peyton," said Jessica.

I just laughed. "Yes, they look like beautiful friends, but they're just glass carousel animals that you named and rode on."

"Oh, Grammy," said Meghan as she pulled me closer to the whale. "They're real! Just look at her—Bella the beluga whale, is so gorgeous and smart and she lived far away before she was brought to the aquarium."

Zach wiggled up next to me and said, "You won't believe where we've been. Tell her Meghan."

Beaming with excitement, Meghan said, "You know the old aquarium you and the ranger told us about, the one Grandma Judy came to see when she was our age? Well," she paused, "It was beautiful. There were six pools with arches that surrounded a large center pool, and inside this pool was Bella the beluga whale. In the smaller pools were Ally the gator, Missy the manatee, Buster the sea lion, and one even had a hammerhead shark that wanted Zach for dinner. I can't wait to talk to Grandma Judy tonight, and tell her all about our adventure in the New York Aquarium."

"Grammy," said Jessica, "Zach rescued a barracuda, and Peyton the penguin told us all about the aquarium that was here in Battery Park in the 1930s."

"Really? That's so silly. What imaginations you have. I'm glad you had fun on this aquatic carousel, but these creatures are made of glass—they're not real or magical," I stressed.

They looked at me like I had gone crazy.

"Grammy," said Zach with a determined look on his face. "They're as real as you and me. We had an adventurous ride on the carousel that took us to the old aquarium that was here in Battery Park."

Trying not to get Zach upset, I asked, "If your adventure is true, how did you get there?"

Looking me straight in the eye, Zach said without missing a beat, "I made a wish to live in an aquarium, and Sparky the electric eel made it come true." Then he added with a stern look on his face, "And they are magical fish too!"

"Oh yeah Grammy, said Jessica, "Peyton the penguin is a famous movie star. In the 1930s they made a movie in the aquarium, so we'll have to Google it when we get back to your apartment," sounding like this was a daily occurrence for her.

"Grammy," said Zach, "remember telling us about those beautiful seahorses over the entrance to the castle this morning?"

"Yes, I do, and I told you to use your imagination and you would be able to see them. Sounds like you have lots of imagination today—maybe a little too much," I laughed.

"Well," said Zach, "They're real and not in my imagination either. Sugar and Spice led the way for us to get back to the carousel from the aquarium after Venus the octopus told us to look closely at the aquarium guide."

"Yes, and Venus is so smart," said Meghan. "She gave us clues to find the golden seahorses. She said we had to go boldly in the direction of trouble—Ally the gator, who tried to keep us from the seahorses.

"She also told us to use our imagination and hearts' desires to get back home," said Jessica.

"And what Peyton didn't tell us about the aquarium when he was our tour guide, we can read about in the guidebook Jessica found," said Meghan. "And there was a note in the guidebook that gave us clues to solve our puzzle, to get us back to Battery Park," she said like a detective.

"And Shelby the chambered nautilus, has swirls on his shell that have a logarithmic spiral pattern," said Jessica.

"A what?" I asked. *This is getting too weird. How would they know this stuff?* I thought.

"Grammy," Jessica continued as she pointed up to the ceiling, "this carousel is designed after Shelby's spiral shell. He's a part of the carousel now too. Just look at it. The walls are the shape of the nautilus shell through the spiraling glass and steel."

Meghan looked up with a sly smile on her face and said, "Grammy, I still have the guidebook in my pocket. Would you like to see it?" She pulled out the old brochure, *The Guide to the New York Aquarium* by Charles Haskins Townsend, along with a single piece of paper with notes written on it.

I couldn't believe what I was seeing. "Where in the world did you get this?" I asked, looking it over, wondering just what had taken place on that carousel.

"We told you, Jessica found it in the aquarium. It helped us arrive where we started," Zach stated firmly.

Then I noticed the name at the top of the booklet: Judith. "Oh no, it can't be great-grandma Judy, can it?" I mumbled to myself. Looking up in disbelief, I noticed for the first time, two golden seahorses adoring the entrance to the carousel.

"You okay, Grammy?" asked Jessica.

Meghan and Jessica took my hands and led me out of the carousel. I stumbled along, but I felt the need to sit down for a while. Before I knew it, we were out in the park where Zelda paraded by.

"Look! Jessica and Meghan," said Zach. "That's Zelda the turkey—she lives here in Battery Park."

"No way," said Meghan. "Turkeys don't live in cities, especially..." But she didn't finish her sentence. "Wait, is she part of our adventure too?"

"No, she was here before we got on the carousel," said Zach with a grin on his face.

"Look over there Grammy. A dancing water fountain," said Jessica.

"It's so hot out; please, can I run through it?" asked Meghan.

"If Jessica and Zach go with you and you don't go any other place, you can," I said.

"I've got to ask you something first," said Zach. "They can go without me for now."

"I'm not sure Jessica wants to come with me, Grammy," said Meghan. "She didn't want Bella to get her wet with her splashes, and ruin her outfit." Then she turned to Jessica and said, "If you like, you can watch me run through the water, so you don't get wet."

"Are you kidding, you bet I'm coming too," said Jessica laughing.

"Don't tell me you're going to get wet now?" Meghan asked.

"Yes I am! I love dancing water fountains, anyway, I don't care if I see a cute boy anymore," said Jessica laughing.

Meghan started laughing too and said, "Let's do cartwheels through the dancing water, that'll be fun!"

They took off not caring if they got soaked.

"Hey Zach," Jessica yelled out. "You've got to come see this. It's a fountain that's shaped like the spiral on your T-shirt and Shelby's shell too! This is such a fantastic park."

"Yeah, Zach, hurry up," said Meghan. Then she said to Jessica as they ran through the granite spiral fountain, "This has been an unbelievable day. I'm so glad we came to see the creepy old castle," she laughed."

Tugging at my arm, Zach asked, "When can I get ice cream? I see the stand right over there."

I laughed, "You've been waiting a long time for ice cream, haven't you? I'll get us some while you run through the fountain with the girls. Go have fun, and stay with your sisters. I'll be right back with the ice cream."

"That would be great. Dancing fountains are really neat, and don't worry Grammy, I'll stick like glue to them." And Zach ran off searching for another adventure.

I thought to myself, *No one's going to believe this magical story, but for Jessica, Meghan, and Zach, it has been an awesome day at the aquarium after all.*

Walking to the ice cream stand, I could hear Zach yelling through the dancing water, "Battery Park is the most wonderful and magical park there is!"

"Yes, Zach," I whispered to myself. "It is a wonderful and magical place. I wish this day could last forever." Just then a breeze blew through the leaves of the trees and I thought I heard it say, "Wishes can come true, in the Magical Battery Park."

BATTERY PARK AQUARIUM: A LITTLE HISTORY

The Aquarium building was constructed by the United States Government between 1807 and 1811 as a fort on the rocks off the tip of Manhattan Island 200 feet from shore. Circular in shape, it was called the South-west Battery and was fully armed with 28 cannons. However, the fort never had an occasion to fire upon the enemy during the War of 1812, and in 1817 was renamed Castle Clinton in honor of DeWitt Clinton, Mayor of New York City and later Governor of New York State.

In 1823 the fort was deeded to New York City, and the following summer a new entertainment center opened at the site. The fort was renamed Castle Garden, and a roof was added in the 1840s. It was connected with Battery Park by a bridge, the intervening space having since been filled in. A newspaper described the interior as a "fanciful garden, tastefully ornamented with shrubs and flowers." In time, a great fountain was installed. The Garden was the setting for concerts, fireworks, and demonstrations of the latest scientific achievements. The gunrooms were decorated with marble busts and painted panoramas, and a promenade was at the top of the Garden wall. Castle Garden served as an opera house and theater and was a great public gathering spot until it closed in 1854.

On August 3, 1855, Castle Garden opened as an immigrant station, becoming the nation's first official immigrant processing center. During the next thirty-four years, over eight million people entered the United States through Castle Garden. Two out of every three immigrants to the United States during this period passed through here. Castle Garden's time as an immigration center ended on April 18, 1890. The Federal government opened Ellis Island in 1892.

The castle was once again remodeled and reopened as the New York City Aquarium in Battery Park on December 10, 1896. The aquarium provided scientific interest, natural history instruction, and cultural improvement. It was one of the show places of New York City. The aquarium became the city's most popular attraction with its exotic fish and beluga whale. Then, as if by magic, in 1941, someone pulled the plug and removed the lid. Today the water, the fish, and the roof have all vanished. The New York City Aquarium relocated to Coney Island in 1957.

Saved from demolition in 1946, the Castle was restored to its original design by the National Park Service. The site reopened in 1975 as Castle Clinton National Monument. Where millions of immigrants once passed, today millions of tourists buy tickets to visit the Statue of Liberty and Ellis Island. The new *SeaGlass* Carousel is located in the southeastern part of Battery Park and is sponsored by the Battery Conservancy, who hopes that this carousel "will not only entertain visitors, but will inspire and educate them."

CASTLE CLINTON THEN AND NOW

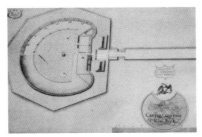

Southwest Battery, 1811-1812

Castle Garden, Entertainment Center 1823-1854

Immigration Processing Center, 1855-1890

New York City Aquarium, 1896-1941

New York City Aquarium, 1901

Castle Clinton today, preserved in its original form

Artist Conception of *SeaGlass*, 2013

Castle Clinton today

CREDITS

1. Southwest Battery, 1811-1812

Courtesy of Castle Clinton National Monument, National Park Service, Manhattan Historic Sites Archive.

2. Castle Garden, 1823-1854

Courtesy of Castle Clinton National Monument, National Park Service, Manhattan Historic Sites Archive. LOC

3. Immigration Processing Center, 1855

Courtesy of Castle Clinton National Monument, National Park Service, Manhattan Historic Sites Archive.

4. New York City Aquarium, 1919

Guide To New York Aquarium by Charles Haskins Townsend, New York Zoological Society, 1919.

5. New York City Aquarium, 1901

Detroit Publishing Company, Prints and Photographs Department, Library of Congress LC D4-13092.

6. Castle Clinton, today

Linda Anderson Lieberman, personal photo.

7. Artist Conception of SeaGlass, 2013

Courtesy of W X Y Architecture + Urban Design, New York, NY.

8. Castle Clinton, today

Linda Anderson Lieberman, personal photo.

Made in the USA
San Bernardino, CA
02 December 2013